SONA SHARMA

VERY BEST BIG SISTER

Other books by Chitra Soundar

A Dollop of Ghee and a Pot of Wisdom
A Jar of Pickles and a Pinch of Justice

SONA SHARMA
VERY BEST BIG SISTER

CHITRA SOUNDAR
Illustrated by JEN KHATUN

WALKER
BOOKS

To my grandfather, who wrote my name on rice kernels

First published in Great Britain 2020 by Walker Books Ltd
87 Vauxhall Walk, London SE11 5HJ

2 4 6 8 10 9 7 5 3 1

Text © 2020 Chitra Soundar
Illustrations © 2020 Jen Khatun

This book has been typeset in Alegreya

Printed and bound by CPI Group (UK) Ltd, Croydon CR0 4YY

British Library Cataloguing in Publication Data:
a catalogue record for this book is available from the British Library

ISBN 978-1-4063-9175-6

www.walker.co.uk

CONTENTS

LIKE THE
BIG SKY

Sona Sharma lives in a large joint family full of happy people who argue sometimes. Relatives come unannounced, the phone rings often and everyone is welcome whatever the time.

These are Sona's people:

Amma – Sona's mum. She is a music teacher and singer. She's always humming a song or listening to music.

Appa – Sona's dad. He works with computers all day and sometimes at night too.

Thatha – Sona's grandfather. He knows a lot of things. And when he doesn't know about something he tells a story about something else.

Paatti – Sona's grandmother. She makes the best sweets in the whole world. She always laughs at Thatha's jokes.

The President – Sona's other grandmother. Sona doesn't know her real name. The President used to be the president of some college, so everyone calls her that still. She lives in the only orange house in the entire neighbourhood, called The Orange.

Joy and Renu – Sona's friends from school. They live a street away and go to school with Sona in an auto-rickshaw.

Mullai – Sona's auto-rickshaw driver. She picks up Sona, Joy and Renu in that order, to drop off at school. In the evening she takes them home – Renu first, Joy next and Sona last. She's never late and recites a lot of Tamil poetry.

Elephant – Sona's best friend. He fits perfectly in her toy bag and her cuddly chair and next to her on her pillow. Sona never goes anywhere without him, except, of course, to school.

Sona and Elephant often play in the garden. Sona's favourite part of the garden is the bench under the shade of the mango trees, next to some banana plants. Elephant loves to hang from the mango tree branches above Sona's head. They read books, make up stories and watch noisy squirrels race around.

On hot summer days Sona waters the hibiscus bushes, the jasmine and curry leaf plants and Paatti's *tulsi* plant, so that she and Elephant can play with the garden hose all afternoon. This is where they were both sitting on a drizzly afternoon after school, thinking about Amma's new baby.

"You're going to be a big sister," Amma had said, the night before. Again. Everyone knew that, even Elephant.

"That's a good thing, no?" asked Elephant, reading Sona's mind.

"I don't know," said Sona. "It was nice being the only sister."

"I know what you mean," said Elephant. "I'm the only elephant in your room."

"I don't want to share," said Sona.

"The room?" asked Elephant.

"Not just the room," said Sona. "I don't want to share Amma, Appa, Thatha, Paatti. Anyone! Even the President. I don't want to share anyone!"

Elephant nodded. He knew that families were not as easy to share as coconuts or bananas.

※

Sona and Elephant came back into the house through the back door. The ceiling fans whirred loudly in the dining room, right outside the kitchen.

The kitchen is the most important room downstairs, where everything important happens. When important things happen, the grown-ups always drink coffee, like they were doing then. Someone was playing the flute on the stereo, but no one seemed to be listening.

Amma was on the sofa, with a book on her lap. But she wasn't reading. Paatti, Thatha and the President were sitting in the wicker chairs. They were talking about the baby. *The baby!* They talked about the baby all the time.

"In our family, it's always girl first, then a boy, just like Lini and Gopi," said Thatha, pointing at a photo of Lini Aunty and Sona's dad, Gopi.

"If the baby kicks on the left," said Paatti, "there's more chance of it being a boy."

"Your nose is swelling, so it could be a girl," said the President.

Amma hummed a song. That was what she did when she was bored.

"I ate a lot of ice cream when I was carrying my first, and it turned out to be a boy," continued the President. "Are you eating sweet burfis or sour mangoes?"

Amma sighed and shrugged.

"If you were at my house, I wouldn't have to ask," said the President.

Sona sat next to Amma on the sofa. The President was always saying that Amma would move to The Orange before the baby was born.

How could Amma move to The Orange when Sona was here?

"It's our custom," said the President. "Or the neighbours might think I'm not a good mother."

"Mother!" said Amma. "No one will think that. Besides, Sona is here and I'd rather stay here with her."

"Sona can come and live in The Orange too."

Sona clutched Elephant tightly. *No, thanks!* The President only made toast for breakfast.

"What do you think, Sona?" asked Amma. "Shall we go to The Orange?"

"No, thanks," said Sona quickly.

The President grunted and said, "Children these days..." She got up and Sona thought she was going home. But she wasn't. She came right back with a piece of paper and tore it in two.

Then she pulled an orange pen out of her enormous orange handbag and wrote on the two bits of paper, folded each one and held them out to Amma.

"Pick one," she said.

"Go ahead, Sona," said Thatha. "Pick the best one."

"One bit of paper says 'boy' and the other says 'girl'," explained Amma. "It's just for fun, to guess about the baby."

Everyone was holding their breath. The only noise in the room came from the ceiling fan.

Sona looked around and thought, *What if I pick the wrong one? That* didn't sound like fun. Sona hesitated on the paper on the left. And

then she thought about the one on the right.
And then she changed her mind again.

"Pick one!" said the President. "Krishna will
help you."

Sona stared at the little bits of paper. She
didn't want to be a big sister, she didn't want
to go to The Orange, and she didn't want a new
baby in the house. *Sona* was the baby of the
family and she wished everything would stay
that way.

Tears welled in Sona's eyes as she threw the
folded papers on
the floor, grabbed
Elephant and ran
upstairs to her room.

Back in her room, Sona walked in circles
like Appa did when he was mad. That made
Elephant dizzy.

Then she pulled out her art box. But she was
in a hurry, so all the little paint jars fell out.

"Is everything OK in
here?" asked Amma as
she opened the door.

Sona threw the art
box down. "Nooooo!
Noooo! Nooo!" she
shouted. "Nothing is
OK. You're not OK. The
President is not OK. The
baby's not OK."

Amma rushed in and held Sona.
"Hey, hey," she said. "Shh!"
"NOT OK!" shouted Sona.
Amma sat on the bed and pulled Sona onto
her lap. Amma's bump nudged Elephant and he
fell onto the floor.

"Why is nothing OK?" asked Amma.

Sona sniffled. "Because everything is changing."

"Like what?"

"Like ... like ... you," said Sona.

"I'm much bigger," said Amma, patting her bump.

"And everyone. No one likes me any more. Everyone just wants the new baby. Even the President wants to take you to The Orange."

Amma held Sona tighter and started to sing. She sang the song Sona used to like when she was inside Amma's tummy. Amma gently rocked Sona as she sang.

"Come to me, bright
golden moon,
slide down the mountains,
jump over streams,
bring me the
scent of valley
blooms.

Come to me, bright golden moon,
walk through the forests, hop over lakes,
bring me the sounds of silent stars.
Come to me, bright golden moon,
Come to me…"

When she'd finished singing, Amma
whispered, "Sona *chellam*, everyone loves you.
Nothing will change that. Even the new baby
will love you."

"You're just saying that," said Sona.

"Let's lie down and pretend we can see the
moon through that
skylight," said Amma,
pointing at the ceiling.
They lay down.
Elephant did too because
he was quite sleepy.

"There are new stars born every day up there, in the sky," said Amma. "The moon and the other stars don't get angry about new stars. Our family is just like that."

"Why don't they get upset with new stars?" asked Sona.

"Because the sky is big enough for many more stars. It always makes room for the new stars. Just like our family. When a new baby is born, we will always make space for it, in our home and in our hearts. Just like the sky – big-hearted and full of beautiful colours."

"Hmm," said Sona.

"In our family, a new star will be born soon, right next to the big star," said Amma.

"I think the big star is you," whispered Elephant. Which Sona already knew.

"We will open our hearts and make a little more space and a lot more love for the new baby. Won't we?"

"Hmm," said Sona.

"Hmm," said Elephant.

That night Sona gazed through her window and thought some more about the big sky and the new baby. "Will I be angry about the baby all the time?" she asked.

"Doesn't Thatha often say *Aaruvadhu Sinam*?" asked Elephant. "Anger is like the milk boiling. It always goes down when it cools."

"You're making me think of Paatti's caramel milk now."

"Mmm," said Elephant.

And soon he and Sona were fast asleep, like the cooling milk turning into yogurt.

TO TURN OR NOT TO TURN

It was Saturday morning. Everyone sat in their usual spots at the table, sipping their coffees. Appa was reading on his tablet. Thatha had his arms outstretched, holding his newspaper, and Sona ducked under them to give him a hug. Amma was already eating breakfast. Paatti was kneading dough. *Maybe she'll make her yummy, puffy* pooris *for lunch*, thought Sona.

"Are you going to have another tantrum?" asked Elephant.

"Why?" asked Sona.

"Because they're talking about the baby again."

Yes, they were. But Sona was still thinking about pooris.

"When do you think we'll have the *namakarna*?" asked Appa. "I need to tell work so that I can take time off."

"Whenever Krishna decrees," said Thatha.

"Sona, you wouldn't remember your naming ceremony," said Amma.

"But we have photos," said Paatti, getting the photo album from the cupboard.

Sona opened the photo album and saw photos of herself as a baby. Elephant was right next to her, even then. Thatha moved closer to Sona to look at the photos too.

"The ceremony takes place ten days after the baby is born," said Paatti.

"What did you call me for those ten days?" asked Sona.

"This and that – sometimes this and sometimes that," said Thatha, chuckling.

"Don't be silly, Thatha," said Sona.

"For the first ten days, a baby is still adjusting to its new family," said Thatha. "When it's ready to meet more people, we invite everyone to the ceremony and give the baby a name."

"What happens in the ceremony?" asked Sona.

She was flipping through the pages.

"Slow down!" said Thatha, turning back a page. "Here, see this one? This is the first step. We spread rice kernels on the floor.

"Then we give new clothes to mother and child, and the father," he continued, pointing at the next photo.

"Each elder then spells out the baby's name on the bed of rice kernels spread on the floor," said Paatti.

"Like we draw on the sand when we go to the beach," said Thatha, pointing at the photo where Paatti was on her knees drawing on the rice.

"After we spell each name," said Thatha, "we'll whisper it into the baby's ear."

"How many names?" asked Sona.

"Usually three," said Thatha. "I think…"

"Thatha and I are picking one," said Paatti.

"The President will pick one," said Amma.

"And third is the one we will use for the baby when it goes to school," said Thatha. "So your parents will pick that."

"Do you remember all your three names?" asked Amma. "I told you once."

Sona shook her head. "No one calls me by the other names."

"I know one," said Appa. "Sona!"

Sona giggled. "Everyone knows that one."

"Kothai," said Paatti, "the name of the great saint and poet."

"And Champa," said Thatha, "the celestial flower."

"Sona, Kothai and Champa," whispered Elephant. "You have three names."

Sona liked being Sona. She turned a few more pages in the album.

"Look, Mullai is in this photo," said Sona.

"Mullai and your amma have been friends since they were in 2nd standard," said Paatti. "Always whispering and being naughty."

"What's this photo?" asked Sona. In the photo, Appa was handing over a tray to Thatha.

"As a thank you, I have to give presents to everyone who helped find a name," said Appa.

Presents! Why hadn't anyone told Sona before?

"So if I help Amma and you find a name, I get a present too?" asked Sona.

Appa nodded. "Of course!" he said.

"There's no time like the present," said Thatha, with a smile. "All of you, go and do something productive. Don't laze around. *Sombi thiriyel*."

"But Saturdays are for lazing around," said Appa, whining.

Sona didn't want to laze around and she went upstairs. "Let's do something productive," she said to Elephant. "Let's find a name for the baby."

"Good idea," said Elephant.

"Names have a habit of getting stuck," said Sona. "So we have to be careful what we choose."

"How come?" asked Elephant.

"If you called me by any other name, I wouldn't turn around."

"I would," said Elephant.

"Why?"

"Because elephants like turning," he said, jumping off the bed and showing off his turns.

Sona laughed. "We need to think of a name for the little baby," she said.

"What is my name?" asked Elephant.

"Elephant," said Sona.

"That's like saying bed, table or banana."

"Actually my bed has a name," said Sona. "It's called Melrose. It was written on the cardboard box."

Elephant hid under the blankets and pretended not to know Sona. He was annoyed with a world where beds had names and elephants didn't.

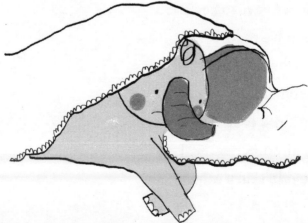

It was almost lunchtime. Sona was hungry. She asked Elephant, "Are you coming down for lunch?"

"I'm not in the mood," said Elephant. "I'm sure Melrose would love to go with you."

Knock-knock!

Amma peeped in through the door. Sona looked up.

"I have to tell you something," Amma began. "The President is right; I should go and stay with her at The Orange until the baby comes."

"I don't want you to go," said Sona. "Why are you going?"

"It's our custom that the baby's mother goes to her mother's house to have the baby," said Amma. "And it's not fair that I went to The Orange before you were born and not for this baby."

"When are you going?"

"Today is auspicious," said Amma. "Today is good. Appa said he'll take me. I'll be there only until the baby comes."

But Sona thought, *What will happen if the President likes the new baby better and keeps Amma at The Orange for ever?*

"We can pack a suitcase for you too."

Sona wasn't sure. The President had breakable glass and unbreakable rules.

"Maybe you'd like to stay here with everyone," said Amma. "For a few days Mullai can drop you off at The Orange after school, until the baby comes."

What did Amma mean when she said "a few"?

Three days or twenty or infinity? What if Amma never came back? Sona didn't know what to do but Thatha always said, "Full stomachs make fine decisions."

Maybe Paatti's pooris would help Sona decide. "I'm hungry," she said.

"Me too," said Amma. "Let's have something to eat."

Amma, Sona and Elephant walked hand in hand down the stairs. Paatti came out of the kitchen with a big smile. "Special pooris coming up for our soon-to-be big sister."

Big sister! Sona was going to be a big sister. Until now she had been all by herself. But not for much longer.

Whether she ate poori or not, the baby was coming. Whether she was going to The Orange or not, Amma was going there.

It wasn't fair! Not even a little bit. Sona didn't feel stretchy or big-hearted like the big sky. She just wanted to hide like an empty new moon in a dark sky.

※

Sona ran out of the back door into the garden. Even her favourite jasmine plant looked droopy in the sun, just like she felt. She sat on the bench, her knees drawn up and her face hidden. Elephant sat next to her, feeling a bit lonely.

"Hey, Sona!" called Thatha.

Startled, Sona turned. She hadn't noticed Thatha weeding the vegetable patch.

"Baby troubles?" asked Thatha.

"How did he know?" asked Elephant. But Thatha always knew how Sona was feeling.

"Amma wants to go to The Orange," said Sona. "What if she doesn't come back?"

"Of course she'll come back,"
said Thatha, getting up. "This is her
home now."

"I wish she didn't have to go to The Orange,"
said Sona.

Thatha came to sit next to Sona and Elephant.

"When your paatti was going to have a baby, she had to go on a train to her mother's house," said Thatha. "I took her and left her there until your dad was born."

"Didn't you miss Paatti?"

"Of course I did," said Thatha. "But Paatti is very special to me. So sometimes I don't mind doing things I don't like, to make her happy."

Sona thought about it. Elephant thought about it.

"Right!" said Thatha. "I'm off to do more weeding. And like the great poet Avvaiyar said,

Thanthai thaai payn: look after your parents. Maybe this is what she meant."

"Is Amma special to you?" asked Elephant.

Sona didn't even need to think for a second. "Yes!" she said.

"So maybe you shouldn't mind her doing things you don't like if it makes her happy?" asked Elephant.

"Maybe," said Sona, going back inside. After a few minutes she said, "Amma! If you really want to go to The Orange, it's OK with me and Elephant. But we will both stay here and help Paatti."

"Sure," said Amma. "You can visit every day after school and tell me all about it."

"I like visiting too," whispered Elephant. But Sona was already busy eating pooris with potatoes on the side. Elephant was relieved too. He didn't want to stay at The Orange either.

SHARING IS CARING

Later that afternoon, Thatha checked his almanac and picked an auspicious time to take Amma to The Orange. The almanac was the book of the moon and stars. It told Thatha about good times and bad times.

Amma gave Sona a big hug. "Bye, Sona, be good," said Amma.

"I'll be back soon," said Appa. "Are you coming with us, Sona?" said Thatha. Sona shook her head. She linked her arms with Paatti and waved goodbye. Sona, the big sister, was going to help with the preparations.

"Come on now," said Paatti. "There are a thousand and eight things to do before the baby comes."

"Like what?" asked Sona.

"We have to get the cradle ready, and the baby clothes and then the rattles."

"That's only three," said Elephant.

"Are we going shopping?" asked Sona. She liked going to the busy market street full of clothes shops, jewellery shops and toy shops. Elephant didn't like shopping much because Sona always left him at home when she went.

"No, no, no," said Paatti. "We still have the old things. Full of good luck and blessings."

"What old things?"

"There's the cradle in the loft, the one we used for your dad, your aunty and you," she replied. "And your clothes and rattles."

"What if the baby wants new stuff?" asked Sona. "What if it's a boy?"

"Baby clothes fit boys and girls the same way," said Paatti. "New clothes will irritate the baby's skin. You wore your cousin's old clothes too."

Sona opened the display case and picked out one of her baby photos. "This is my favourite outfit," she said. She was wearing a white dress with blue stars on it.

"I hope we still have it," said Paatti.

Inside the tiny room under the staircase was a brown leather suitcase. Paatti brought it out and wiped it with a cloth.

"Can I open it?" asked Sona.

Sona snapped the clasps open and lifted the lid. On top was a bag full of rattles.

"Thatha and I gave you this silver one," said Paatti. "And the President brought this wooden one back from Kerala."

"There are many elephants in Kerala," said Elephant.

"What about the green one?" asked Sona. The green rattle was full of cowrie shells. It made noises of the sea.

"I think your parents got that at Marina Beach," said Paatti. "It was your favourite."

"Are you going to give the baby all my stuff?" asked Sona.

"A hoarded fruit goes rotten," said Paatti. "Do you remember the rocking horse? One of your cousins gave that to you."

"But..."

Sona shook the green rattle.

"Rattles don't rot," she said.

Paatti laughed. Sona looked inside the clothes bag.

"Look, Paatti, I found it," said Sona, holding up the white baby dress with blue stars.

"Wonderful!" said Paatti. "We can take a matching photo of the baby, just like yours."

Sona held the dress behind her back. "But I don't want to give this to the baby," she said.

Paatti shut the suitcase and smiled. "Maybe you'll share it when you're ready."

Paatti never asked Sona to do things she didn't want to do. Just the opposite of the President, Sona thought.

In her room, Sona carefully folded the white dress with blue stars and held it to her face. It was soft, like Amma's hug.

"Aaachoo!" sneezed Elephant. "It stinks. It's rotting already, like Paatti said."

"No, it isn't," said Sona. "It smells like baby me and a bit of Amma."

"I don't think it will fit you any more."

"It doesn't matter," said Sona as she put the dress into her special box for special things. "It's mine. I'm going to use it."

Appa and Thatha soon returned from The Orange. Paatti handed them each a cup of coffee and a list of things to do.

"You're a hard taskmaster," groaned Appa.

"Come on, Sona," said Thatha. "Let's help Appa. As the wise poet once said, *"Paruvathe Payir Sey.* Let's do things at the right time."

A messy corner of Appa and Amma's bedroom was full of books, old computers, old files, lots of old keyboards, games consoles and a huge pile of old shoes.

Every time Appa said "No" or "Not that", Paatti said, "A tidy room reflects a tidy mind." So, with a lot of *aahs* and *oohs*, and frowns and shrugs, Appa created a big pile of things to give away, another pile to recycle and a small pile of "I'll never, ever, ever throw this away."

Now there was space for the baby in their room.

"How about me?" asked Sona. "Can I sleep with you and Amma and the baby too?"

"Will you fit in the cradle?" asked Appa.

"I will," whispered Elephant.

"No, thanks," said Sona. "I like to sleep in my own bed, and look at the stars at night."

"Me too," said Elephant.

Then Appa climbed into the loft to get the cradle, while Thatha and Sona held the ladder.

"Elephants don't like climbing ladders," said Elephant. "It makes us dizzy."

Appa wasn't at all dizzy. Sona and Appa went to clean the cradle in the back garden while Elephant watched.

"I'll hold the hose," Sona said, while Appa scrubbed.

"When I was just four, I helped Thatha clean the cradle to give to Lini Aunty," said Appa.

"But it was yours?"

"I was too big for it then, wasn't I?" said Appa.

"I even shared all my clothes and then my books
and comics with my sister."

Finally the cradle was wiped, dried, carried
and set up next to Amma's side of the bed. It
was red and white and made of wicker. "See, it
moves," said Appa, rocking the basket between
the two stands.

"Like a swing," said Sona.

Paatti sat down on the floor next to the cradle, her legs stretched out.

"Yes, if it stopped swinging, you would scream like a *raakshasi*," said Appa, chuckling. "You were a fearsome creature."

Sona giggled.

"Maybe you too can help with the baby," said Thatha.

Sona's smile disappeared. She stepped over Paatti's legs and went to her room.

"Aw! That's bad luck," said Paatti, folding her legs. Even though Sona knew it was bad luck, she didn't say sorry. She didn't want to take turns rocking the baby. She didn't want to share her cradle or her clothes or her rattles. She was not as nice as Appa and that made her even more angry. Her heart didn't feel stretchy like the big sky.

Knock-knock!

Appa peeped in. "I'm sorry I called you a raakshasi," he said.

Sona looked up. She wasn't mad about that.

"I know a new baby means a lot of new things," said Appa, coming in and sitting on the bed.

"Why did you share your things with your sister?" asked Sona.

"In those days Thatha didn't have a lot of money," said Appa. "We shared all our things.

All my school uniforms were second-hand, from my cousin."

"Were you poor?" asked Sona.

"We weren't short of love and sharing," said Appa. "Just money."

"Are we poor?" asked Sona.

"Only if we don't love each other," said Appa. "As a family, we'll never run out of love."

Elephant nodded. He didn't want to run out of coconuts or love.

"I love you, Appa," said Sona.

"I love you too!" said Appa. "I want to ask you a favour."

"What is it?"

"Your amma is looking for boy names for the baby," said Appa.

"I'm going to pick a girl's name," he continued. "Will you help me make a list of names to choose from?"

"Yes!" said Sona.

"Yes!" said Elephant.

Because as Thatha often said, *Iyalvadhu Karavel* was their family's motto. Always help as best you can.

NAMES HAVE STORIES

When Sona came downstairs the next morning, Thatha's "On Time Every Time" pendulum clock said she was ten minutes early. Her bag was full of books for school but her head was full of *no ideas* to help with girls' names for the baby.

Thatha was in his usual easy chair, busy flipping through his diary.

"Thatha!" called Sona. "How did you pick my name?"

"Is it like picking coconuts?" whispered Elephant.

"Good morning to you too," said Thatha. "That's a special story."

Thatha looked like he was in a storytelling mood. Sona was in a story-listening mood. So was Elephant. She quickly sat in front of Thatha on the stool, with Elephant by her side.

Thatha cleared his throat and began.

"There was once a place by the sea, where sands counted time and waves sang to the moon, and a baby was born at the crack of dawn. She had enormous eyes, lots of hair and a big smile. She saw everything around her and she knew everyone loved her."

"Hmm," said Sona.

"Her parents wanted her grandfather to pick a name for the baby," he continued. "Her grandfather knew that it had to be special. A name that sparkled and shone, just like her."

"Hmm," said Paatti, who had come to listen.

"So the grandfather pondered all morning and all night. He thought about diamonds and rubies, the moon and the stars. But none of those felt special enough."

"And then?" asked Sona.

"The sad grandfather sat next to his happy wife on the terrace. His wife gave him a glass of cold *badam* milk, which was the same colour as the moon. As the grandfather turned to look at his wife under the moonlight," said Thatha, "he realized the sparkliest person ever was his wife."

"Is sparkliest a real word?" asked Paatti.

"You're real," said Thatha.

Paatti chuckled.

"Then?" asked Sona.

"So he decided his granddaughter would be named Kanaka, like her grandmother," he said. "But wouldn't two Kanakas in one house be confusing?"

"So what did you do?" asked Sona.

"It was the night before the naming ceremony," he said. "Time was running out."

Sona gasped.

"Suddenly the grandfather yelled EUREKA!"

Sona giggled. The best bit of the story must be coming.

"The next morning he came down with a dance in his step, a smile on his face and his heart full of love. He called the little baby girl Sona. Sona – his shining gold."

Elephant was confused. He didn't get how Thatha went from Kanaka to Sona.

"Kanaka means gold; Sona also means gold," said Paatti. "Our names have the same meaning. They are synonyms!"

Sona sighed. That was a beautiful story indeed. And Elephant sighed too. He wasn't confused any more.

Beep-beep! Mullai was here. Sona and Thatha and Elephant went hand in hand to the auto-rickshaw.

"Bye, Sona," said Thatha.

"Bye, Sona," said Elephant.

It was time for school.

Everyone at school was curious about the baby too.

"Is the baby born yet?" asked Miss Rao, Sona's teacher.

"Not yet," said Sona.

"She doesn't know if it'll be a boy or a girl," said Joy to Miss Rao.

"The doctor is not allowed to say," said Miss Rao. "You can only find out when the baby is born."

"A suspense!" said Renu.

"Amma is finding boy names and I'm helping Appa find girl names."

"That's a big job," said Joy.

"I have an idea," said Renu.

During morning break, Sona, Joy and Renu trooped to the library.

"Listen to this," said Renu, reading from *Great Women of India*. "Ismat, Kamala, Kamini."

Sona liked Ismat and she wrote it down. Then Sona found five more names in the comic books:

- Jhansi fought in a battle
- Ahilya was a wise queen
- Amrita was a painter
- Anasuya was a leader
- Captain Prem was a pilot

In total, Sona had six names. "I think Appa will be happy with this list," she said.

That afternoon, when Mullai came to pick them up from school, Sona, Joy and Renu told her about the list.

"Maybe one day they'll do a book about me," said Sona.

"And me too," said Renu. "I'll become an astronaut."

"I'm going to be a polar scientist," said Joy.

Mullai pulled the lever to start the auto-rickshaw. Then she eased into traffic, her arms waving out to signal to a motorbike that was trying to overtake her.

"You haven't seen the baby yet," said Mullai. "How do you know which name will fit?"

"Thatha said my name is special because it means the same as Paatti's name."

"Shouldn't you pick a special name that means something to you?" asked Mullai. "Like Thatha did?"

"Aww!" cried Sona, Renu and Joy. What were they going to do now?

Time was running out. That evening, just after dinner, when Appa and Sona were getting ready to go to The Orange, the phone rang. *Tring-tring-tring!* Who could be calling?

BABY IS THE CENTRE OF THE UNIVERSE

The phone was ringing. Amma was calling Appa urgently.

"Stay here, Sona," said Appa. "I'm going to get Amma from The Orange and take her to the hospital."

"She's going to have the baby," gushed Paatti. "Drive carefully."

"Best of luck!" shouted Thatha and then mumbled a prayer.

"Stop worrying," said Paatti, but she was lighting a lamp and saying a prayer too.

"Are you scared?" asked Sona.

"Not scared, my almond moon," said Thatha. "Just praying that the baby is healthy."

Sona and Elephant wanted to pray too. Sona mumbled the *Hanuman Shlok* that the President had taught her. "This is the prayer when you're not feeling brave," she had said.

Elephant mumbled a prayer too. "I'm praying to Ganesha," he said. "The god of all elephants. He's the best."

Thatha texted everyone. Then he checked his phone for messages. Then he checked that it was charged. Then he checked it had signal.

Ding-ding! His phone beeped all evening.

He paced from gate to garden, from front door to back, all the while mumbling prayers.

"Sit down," said Paatti.

The TV was on, but no one watched it.

Thatha added more oil to the lamp in front of the Krishna sculpture at the altar. *"Sarvam Krishnam Samarpayami,"* he kept chanting.

Elephant wanted to know what it meant. Sona did too.

"Thatha is praying to Krishna, and asking Krishna to take care of everything," explained Paatti.

Sona stood next to Thatha and chanted with him.

Elephant whispered, "Don't worry, Krishna always helps Thatha."

The phone rang again. First it was Lini Aunty calling from London, then Uncle Prasad called from California.

Mullai had called round and sat down with Paatti. "There's nothing to worry about," she said. "I'm just waiting to find out if it's a boy or a girl."

"Boy or girl, as long as mother and baby are fine," said Paatti. "Sona, why don't you go to bed? It's getting late."

"I want to find out too," said Sona. Sona hadn't found any names to share with Appa. What if it was a girl and they had no names for the baby? What if the baby was always called Baby?

Suddenly the phone rang again.

"Hello," said Thatha. "Is there any news? Has Nidhi had the baby?"

Appa's voice shouted, "We have a little baby girl and Nidhi is OK too, just tired!"

A baby girl?! Sona ran over to Thatha and looked over his shoulder. She could see Appa holding the baby in his arms. Amma was next to him, smiling. The baby was tiny with her fists closed and eyes shut. Her skin was pinkish and her toes curled.

"We'll be back at The Orange in the morning," said Appa, handing the baby to Amma.

"Love you, Sona," said Amma, blowing a kiss and waving at Sona.

The baby opened her eyes, as if she wanted to look at Sona too.

That night Sona couldn't sleep. She had a baby sister. Tiny and beautiful. She felt extra happy, like the big sky with a new star.

"That must be love," said Elephant.

Sona had to pick an extra-special name, for an extra-special baby sister.

The next day, at school, Sona told Joy and Renu all about the baby. "She is so little," said Sona, "and wrinkly."

"You *have* to find a special name, quick!" said Joy.

"It's not that easy," said Renu.

"Shh!" said Miss Rao.

Sona couldn't concentrate. She kept thinking about Amma and the baby and the baby's name.

That evening, Mullai dropped Sona off at The Orange. "Bye, Sona," shouted Mullai, "tell your amma to take rest."

Paatti, Thatha, Appa – everyone was at The Orange. Amma was asleep in the spare room, with the baby next to her.

The President was sitting on a chair near the bed, reading. "Shh!" she said, putting a finger to her lips.

But Amma must have heard Sona come in. She sat up and said, "Hey, Sona, I missed you so much."

Sona gave Amma a big hug. "I missed you too, loads and loads," she said. "I even recited the Hanuman Shlok and prayed with Thatha that you and the little baby would be OK."

"Good girl," said the President, with a rare smile.

"I knew you would pray for me," said Amma. "I can always count on you, my big star."

"When are you coming home?" asked Sona. "Will the baby come too?"

"Of course the baby is coming," said Paatti. "Don't you worry!"

"Soon, maybe tomorrow around lunchtime," said Amma. "We can't wait."

Sona leaned in over Amma to look at the baby. She had a tiny nose and long eyelashes, just like hers.

That extra-happy feeling came back again.

"My little sister," whispered Sona. She stayed close to the baby all evening.

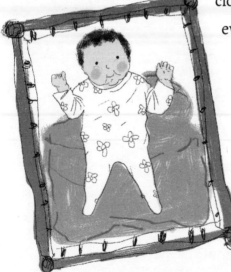

"Who does she look like, Sona?" asked Paatti.

"Does she look like me?" asked Sona, with a shy smile.

"We won't know for a few days," said the President.

When it was bedtime, Sona didn't want to leave.

"Do you want to sleep here?" Amma asked.

Sona wanted to say yes. But she suddenly remembered that Elephant was still back in her room. "Elephant will be scared to sleep alone," she said.

"OK," said Amma. "We'll be there tomorrow as soon as possible."

As they walked back home, Sona asked, "Thatha, when is the naming ceremony?"

"Either the tenth or the twelfth day from last night," he said. "I need to check with the priest."

Sona opened her hands and tried to count the tenth day. But she kept getting muddled.

"I think it might be a Saturday," said Thatha.

"Yay!" squealed Sona. "Then I won't have school."

"We'll declare a national holiday if it's not a Saturday," joked Thatha.

"After all, you're the big sister," said Paatti.
"We can't do the ceremony without you."

Sona smiled. She was the baby's big sister.
For ever and ever and ever. Being a big sister
was a big job and the big sister's first job was to
find a special name.

When Amma and the baby came home, things
were different. Sona wasn't sure if it was good
different or bad different.

Everyone was busy all the time.

"Paatti, can I get a snack?" asked Sona.

"Just a minute," said Paatti. "I need to change
the baby's sheet."

And then Paatti forgot. Sona got a *murukku*
from the snack box by herself.

"Thatha, can I tell you a joke?" asked Sona.

"When I get back from the shops," said
Thatha, rushing off with a list of things to buy
for the naming ceremony.

The phone rang often and it was always
Amma's friends or Paatti's friends or the

President's friends asking about the baby.

The President spent most of her time in Amma's room. She was always ordering everyone about saying totally opposite things.

"Open the window, the baby needs fresh air." "Close the window, the mosquitoes will bite the baby." "Switch on the fan, the baby will sweat." "Cover her head, she might catch the chill."

Sona wanted to see the baby over and over again. She went to the room to look when Amma was sleeping.

The baby was awake in the cradle. Sona gently rocked it.

"I think she likes it," whispered Sona.

The baby watched Sona with her marble-black eyes. Sona touched the baby's fingers and the baby gurgled and grabbed Sona's finger. The baby's nails were a little sharp but Sona didn't mind. That extra-special feeling came back again.

That night, after everyone went to sleep, Elephant said, "Tell me about the baby again."

"She has big eyes, a small nose and a tiny mouth," said Sona. "Her fingers held on to mine really tightly. I think she likes me."

"How do you know that?"

"I just know," said Sona. "That's how big sisters are."

ARE YOU READY, SONA?

The ceremony was just a day away. Thatha
announced that he had already chosen a name.
The President said she had chosen one even
before the baby was born. Amma and Appa
hadn't decided on one yet.

"Isn't that a good thing?" asked Elephant.
"That means you can still help Appa find a name."

"I haven't found any special names," said Sona.

"Yet," said Elephant.

That morning before school, Amma asked Sona, "Which skirt do you want to wear for the ceremony tomorrow?"

Sona rifled through all her silk blouses and skirts.

"What's the baby wearing?"

"The white one with blue stars," said Amma. "The one you wore for your naming ceremony."

"But that's mine," whispered Sona. "Why didn't you ask me first?"

"I'm sorry," said Amma. "I should have. I keep forgetting important things. Paatti calls it baby brain."

Sona didn't say anything.

"OK," said Amma. "We'll just put her in another old dress."

Still Sona didn't say anything.

"What will you wear?" asked Amma. Sona picked a blue silk skirt with a pink blouse.

At school, Sona didn't feel like playing with Renu and Joy. She didn't even finish her lunch.

"You're awfully quiet today," said Mullai, dropping her off at home that afternoon.

Sona just shrugged.

⁂

That evening, the house got very busy.

Phones rang. The grocery shop delivered Thatha's list of things. Then the vegetables arrived: tomatoes, green bananas, stringy beans, yellow cabbage, green chillies and coriander. The lady from the flower stall brought a bundle of jasmine flowers and a bag of pink roses. A cleaning lady came to dust the house and clean the bronze pots for cooking the feast the next day.

All of a sudden, a big bullock cart pulled up.
Two big white bulls with bells around their
necks stopped in front of the gate. The cart was
filled with poles and bundles of coconut thatch
and folded chairs.

"Sir! Sir!" a man called.

Sona looked out of the window. "You're not
sir," said Elephant.

Thatha and Appa opened the gate and
pointed at the terrace. From out of the cart the

men pulled the poles, coconut thatch and folding chairs. Appa went up to the terrace and Sona and Elephant followed him upstairs to watch.

"What are they doing?" asked Sona.

"They're going to put up a *pandhal*," said Appa. "We'll have the ceremony here on the roof terrace."

"A tent?" asked Sona. "Like a circus?"

"Like a tent but with a flat roof," said Appa.

"Then it's not a tent," said Elephant.

"It's a pandhal," said Sona.

After the pandhal went up, the men unfolded and arranged the chairs. Elephant sat in one of the chairs and watched Sona help.

Then, downstairs to the garden, the men chopped two banana plants with the flowers hanging and tied them on each side of the front gate.

"Thatha!" called Sona.

"Not now, my shining star," said Thatha.

So Sona went to Paatti, who was making coconut burfis, and asked about the banana plants.

"We tie the banana plants in front of the house, so everyone will know we're having a ceremony and they are welcome to attend. We must always share our joys."

"Poor banana plant," said Sona. Elephant was sad too.

"The banana plant is a symbol of love," said Paatti. "If you cut the stem, it grows back. When you share your love, it grows again."

"I'll never run out of bananas then," said Elephant. "Or love."

That made Sona think.

Charu Aunty, the helper, was sitting on the floor chopping vegetables.

"Can I help too?" asked Sona.

"Do you want to peel the ends off the beans?" asked Paatti.

Elephant thought it was best to eat beans without peeling the ends or the stringy bits. But people and elephants were very different.

"Have the parents chosen a name for the baby?" asked Charu Aunty.

Sona looked up. Her heart was beating fast. Had her parents picked a name already?

"I think they have," said Paatti.

Appa had picked a name without her help. That wasn't fair.

"But you don't have any names to give Appa," reminded Elephant.

Sona's eyes teared up. Everything was going wrong. First she hadn't found even one special name. Then she had refused to share her dress with the baby. Everything was Sona's fault. She dropped the beans she was trimming, grabbed Elephant and ran to the garden.

The jasmine buds were opening up and their fragrance spread through the garden.

"If the baby doesn't have a special name, it'll be my fault."

"Maybe," said Elephant.

"I don't think I'm going to be a good big sister after all," said Sona.

"Maybe," whispered Elephant sadly.

"I give up, I give up, I give up!" shouted Sona.

"You can't give up," said Thatha gently as he sat next to Sona. Sona pulled her knees up and hid her face.

"Whatever it is you were thinking of doing, don't give up," said Thatha. *"Ookamadhu kaividale."*

Sona shrugged.

"Look there," said Thatha.

Sona looked there. Elephant looked too.

"What is it, Thatha?" asked Sona. It was dark. The canopy of mango and guava trees didn't let much moonlight come through.

"The moon is far away and the stars are behind clouds," said Thatha. "The moon can't light up every garden and every forest."

Sona looked up. She could hardly see the moon. But what were those little flickers of light? They came and went, like sparkles. Sona pointed at the flickers of light moving through the trees.

"That's the firefly," said Thatha. "It flaps its wings to make light in this dark night." The firefly glowed as it went around the garden.

"It's not as bright as the moon," said Sona.

"Even though it isn't as big as the moon," said Thatha, "it still gives out its best sparkle, doesn't it? It never gives up."

Another firefly flew past Sona and Elephant. "Can you see two of them now?" said Thatha. "Like you and your little sister, sparkling together."

Later that evening, after dinner, Sona and Elephant sat down to read a book. Elephant couldn't read, so he was just looking at the pictures. Sona couldn't read because she was thinking about the baby.

"I didn't help Appa find a name," said Sona suddenly.

"Is that a line in the book?" asked Elephant.

"I want to help," said Sona. "Maybe I should share my dress with her."

"But it's yours," said Elephant.

"But it won't fit me any more," said Sona. "And I want the baby to be beautiful in the photos too."

"You're a very good big sister," said Elephant.

When Amma came to tuck Sona and Elephant in for the night, Sona said, "I think the baby will look very beautiful in our dress."

"I think so too," said Amma, giving Sona a kiss on her forehead.

Sona smiled as she fell asleep. And that night in Sona's dreams, two fireflies flew through the trees, sparkling brightly.

EXTRA HAPPY, EXTRA SPECIAL

It was the morning of the naming ceremony.
Sona was in her room with Elephant and
together they watched the guests arrive.
Neighbours dressed in silk were making their
way to Sona's house. Some carried brown
envelopes, some brought flowers or fruits.

"They're all bringing gifts," said Sona.

"For me?" asked Elephant.

"Not for us," said Sona. "For the baby."

"Are you bringing a gift too?" asked Elephant.

Should she? How come no one had told her about it? Sona hadn't found the baby a name. She hadn't bought any gifts either. She must be the worst big sister in the whole world.

"The baby won't know," said Elephant. "She hasn't seen many big sisters yet."

"I'll know," said Sona. "I'm a big sister."

What was she going to do?

"You can make one," said Elephant. "Like you did for Amma's birthday."

What a terrific idea! Elephants are indeed clever, thought Sona.

But before she could think of a gift to make, Amma came in with the baby. Amma looked beautiful in her golden sari with the dark blue border. The baby was wearing Sona's naming dress and she had a gold chain around her neck. She was crying.

"Do you want some cereal before they serve the special breakfast to everyone?" asked Amma.

Sona shook her head. No time for that. She had to think of a present. And she wanted to eat the special breakfast. Not cereal.

"Please get ready quickly," said Amma. "I've got to feed the baby so she won't cry during the ceremony."

Sona nodded. Elephant nodded too.

"Come to the terrace before the motorbike priest gets here," warned Amma. "If we're late, he'll tell us the Gandhi story of punctuality, again."

Sona giggled. "I like that Gandhi story."

"You like all stories," said Elephant, and he was right.

Sona pulled out her art box.

"What are you making?" asked Elephant.

"Wait for it," said Sona, pulling out her paints and an empty jar. She turned away from Elephant as if it was a secret and mixed her paint.

Then she went to her parents' room and turned on Amma's hairdryer to dry the paint.

Knock-knock!

Sona quickly hid everything under the pillow.

Paatti walked in with a glass of milk. "Here, at least drink this," said Paatti. "You can't stay hungry till they serve the special ceremony breakfast."

Sona gulped down the milk and wiped her milk moustache.

Paatti waited for Sona to put on her blue silk skirt and pink blouse. Then she combed Sona's hair into a plait and pinned a string of jasmine flowers.

"You look beautiful," said Paatti. "Are you coming upstairs now? The priest will be here soon."

"Soon, soon, very soon," said Sona. "I've something to finish."

"Don't be late," said Paatti. "Late peacocks miss the rain."

Elephant looked through the window. Was it going to rain?

Just then the priest arrived with two honks. He was on his red motorbike and wearing a red helmet. Paatti rushed out.

Sona hurriedly filled a gift bag with special things from her special box. Her presents would be the best ever for her best ever sister, even if she hadn't found a special name yet. Upstairs, under the pandhal, two big fans whooshed. The camera was set up next to the laptop so all the family in California and London could watch. Sona hid her bag of presents behind the laptop stool and sat next to Amma and Appa with Elephant.

The President, Thatha and Paatti sat opposite them. The priest was giving orders to everyone. Guests scurried like ants and got to their spots before the chanting started. The priest settled on his wooden seat and chanted a mantra that Appa repeated.

Appa kept adjusting the camera.

"Focus on the prayers," said Thatha.

The baby was quiet. She had her big eyes open and looked around. When Sona leaned into her, the baby got hold of her hair.

Soon the chanting was over. "Turn on the good music," said the priest, and Appa leaned in and turned on the devotional music on his laptop.

"Low volume, please," said the priest. "We don't want to scare the baby."

The baby made a noise as if she agreed.

"Now's the time to name the child so she brings honour and joy to your family," said the priest.

Amma brought the baby forward and handed her over to Paatti.

"What is the first name?" asked the priest. "To uphold the father's family honour."

"Veda," said Thatha. Thatha and Paatti whispered the name into the baby's ear. Appa drew the name on the bed of rice kernels.

"It means, 'the sacred word'," said the priest loudly.

"Second name?" asked the priest. "To honour the mother's side."

"Alamu," said the President, whispering into the baby's ear. "It's the name of the baby's great-grandmother."

The President erased Veda with her palm and then spelled *Alamu* on top of it.

Just one name was left and Sona knew it would not be the one she had found. Because she hadn't found any special names. Not even now.

"The third name?" asked the priest. "The name that will honour the child."

Sona hid her face in Elephant's trunk. Her head was empty of names. She couldn't think of anything special.

Appa put his arm around Sona and whispered, "Look up, Amma picked a good name. It means angel."

Sona looked up reluctantly. Amma was tracing the letters A-D-I-T-I in English and then in Tamil on the bed of rice kernels. Then Amma and Appa together whispered into the baby's ear, "Aditi."

Friends and relatives called out "Aditi" from across the terrace.

"Everyone's happy," said Elephant.

"Not me," said Sona. "I didn't find her a special name. And now the ceremony is finished."

The smell of *vada* and *payasam* wafted from downstairs. Sona had failed in her first job as a big sister.

"Are we done?" asked Appa.

"Not yet," said the priest. "Now we need to give her the name everyone will call her at home. The name filled with love and affection."

"What, a fourth name?" asked Amma, looking at Thatha.

"But we chose only three!" said Appa. "That's what the priest told us last time."

"Maybe the old priest was wrong," muttered Thatha. "He was always forgetting things."

The motorbike priest chuckled. "Trust me," he said. "I've a Masters degree in scriptures. Passed with distinction too. You should always give four names. An even number makes for a smooth life. Quick, quick. The clock is ticking."

Sona twisted Thatha's hand and checked his watch. It was ticking.

"Sona might have one!" said Mullai.

"Quick!" said the priest. "We have just two minutes left in the auspicious hour."

"Didn't you make a list at school?" asked Thatha.

"I threw it out because the names weren't special," said Sona.

"Close your eyes and think about beautiful things," said Thatha. "You'll remember."

"Don't go to sleep," warned Elephant.

Sona closed her eyes. She couldn't recall any of the names she had on the list.

She thought about the determined fireflies that Thatha had showed her. So she scrunched her eyes tight and tried again.

"Sona..." nudged Amma.

Sona opened her eyes and smiled. Yes! She had it. A name just popped into her head like a flash of light.

"Minmini," she whispered into the baby's ears. Little Minmini looked at Sona with her big eyes.

"Please say it loudly too," said Amma. "So I can write it."

"Minmini," said Sona. "The firefly that sparkles in the dark."

"That's beautiful," said Appa.

"Good job!" said Mullai.

Thatha smiled at Sona. "Sona and Minmini, my two favourite girls in the whole world, the two sparkliest fireflies that shine like stars."

"What about me?" asked Paatti.

Everyone laughed.

Appa stood up with two yellow cloth bags. First he gave a gift to Thatha and Paatti and fell at their feet for blessings.

Then Appa gave the second gift to the President. The President touched Appa's and Amma's heads with a blessing.

"What about me?" asked Sona. "I picked a name too."

"Of course you did," said the priest. "You saved the day."

"Can we get you a present later?" asked Appa. "You surprised us."

"You can even choose it," said Amma.

Sona nodded. "And one for Minmini too?"

"Big sister's already looking out for baby sister," said Mullai, laughing.

Then it was time for the guests to give presents to the baby.

"I have some presents for Minmini too," said Sona, grabbing the bag from behind the stool.

"What's in it?" asked Paatti.

Sona held up the green rattle with cowrie shells. "It was my favourite one," she said.

"Now it's for Minmini."

Paati came over and hugged her. "Sona Sharma, you're the best big sister ever," she said. "I'm so proud of you."

"There's more," said Sona, pulling out the glass jar. "I made a firefly lantern for Minmini. So she'll know why she got her special name."

"That's beautiful," said Appa.

"Sona is the best big sister in the whole world," said Amma.

Elephant nodded. Indeed she was.

⁂

That afternoon, after the ceremony breakfast, the grown ups were in the living room, drinking coffee and talking about the ceremony. Minmini was in her cradle in her parents' room. Appa was napping near by on the bed.

"Shh!" said Elephant.

Sona tiptoed closer. Appa had already put up the firefly lantern in front of the cradle, so Minmini could watch it glow in the dark at night. She was wearing the white dress with blue stars and holding her green rattle.

The baby was awake, looking right at her.

"I have a doubt," said Elephant. "Did your parents give you only three names?"

"Hmm," said Sona.

"You need a fourth one too," he said.

Sona thought for a moment. "My fourth name is Akka," she said. "Akka means big sister. That's what Minmini will call me."

The baby blew a raspberry.

"Then what about me?" asked Elephant.

"She can't call you Akka, because you're a boy," said Sona.

"Not that," said Elephant. "I want four names too."

But before Sona could answer, the baby put her hand out and caught Sona's little finger.

"She loves me," said Sona.

"She loves me too," said Elephant.

Minmini gave a little gurgle.

"And we both love her," said Sona.

NEW WORDS TO EXPLORE IN THIS STORY

akka – big sister

badam – almond

burfi – rectangular or diamond-shaped sweets made with sugar and flour or sugar and coconut

chellam – dear

Ganesha – the elephant-headed god

Hanuman Shlok – a prayer usually written in Sanskrit

Krishna – a Hindu god

murukku – a spirally crispy snack made of lentil flour

namakarna – the naming ceremony

pandhal – a marquee made of coconut thatch

payasam – a milk pudding that you can drink

poori – deep-fried puffy bread eaten with a side of potatoes or with chickpeas

raakshasi – a mythical demon, a very fearsome creature

2nd standard – Year 2

Tamil – the language spoken by Sona and her family

tulsi – the holy basil plant, named after goddess Tulsi

vada – a savoury doughnut made of lentil batter

Chitra Soundar is originally from the culturally colourful India, where traditions, festivals and mythology are a way of life. As a child, she feasted on generous portions of folktales and stories from Hindu mythology. As she grew older, she started making up her own stories. Chitra now lives in London, cramming her little flat with storybooks of all kinds.

❈

Jen Khatun's work is inspired by the natural world, the books on her shelves and the hidden magical moments found in everyday life. She says, "Being of Bangladeshi heritage meant that Chitra's story reminded me of the close bonds, traditions and memories of my family life. As a grown up, I cherish every profound life-teaching my family gifted me; they have made me who I am today."